Isabella's Wish

by Stephen Perez

ISBN: 978-1-969865-03-9 (sc)
ISBN: 978-1-969865-04-6 (e)

Rev. date: 09/25/2025

There was a very well-kept secret land high up in the mountains. No one even knew it was there, and the ruler of this land wanted to keep it that way. Queen Isabella was a strict but very kind ruler. She loved the people of her land and wanted only good things for them.

She went out among them every day to say hello and ask how they were doing. All the people in the kingdom truly loved and respected her. They were glad that she was their queen.

But there was one thing missing in her life—a king. Someone who could help her rule the land. This was her one and only wish: to find someone to be her king.

Whenever the people in her land needed something, she sent out a party to go down into the valley to retrieve it. Most of the time, though, they simply made what they needed right there within the kingdom. They grew vegetables and raised their own animals. Hardly anyone ever left, and everyone seemed content to live there for the rest of their lives.

There were no crimes. Everyone got along. It was a very special place to live, indeed.

Sometimes, Isabella would take a walk through the garden. It was a large garden filled with flowers and towering trees. One day, she was outside enjoying the fresh air and talking to herself.

mai's CABBAG

As she spoke, she suddenly heard a voice.

"Hello," said the voice.

Isabella fell silent and listened, thinking that her imagination was playing tricks on her.

"Helloooo," the voice said again.

This time, Isabella felt a chill of fear run down her spine.

"Who's there?" she asked.

"It's me!" said the voice, coming from a tree.

Isabella looked up and saw an owl staring down at her.

"Owl," said Isabella, "are you the one talking to me?"

"Of course," said the owl.

Terrified at his answer, Isabella turned to run away.

"Please don't go!" the owl pleaded. "If you listen, I can explain everything."

"Hmmm," said Isabella. "You'd better start talking."

"My name is Ferdinand," said the owl. "I am the king of the land in the valley south of here. Everything had been going so well for us until one day, a wicked witch arrived and began causing trouble. When I tried to have her arrested, she put a spell on me! She turned me into an owl and told me that the only way to break the spell was to find someone with a pure heart. The last thing she said was, 'Good luck with that,' and then she disappeared.

"I overheard some of your people talking about you when they came down to the valley for supplies. They had nothing but good things to say about you. So, I thought I would come see if you could help me break this spell."

"Well, what would you need from me?" asked Isabella.

"If you truly have a pure heart," said the owl, "all you must say is, "I relieve you of this spell."

Isabella hesitated but decided to give it a try.

"I relieve you of this spell," she said.

Nothing happened.

"I don't know what went wrong," said the owl. "Maybe I need to be on the ground, so I don't fall out of the tree."

He flew down and landed in front of her.

"Please try again!" he begged.

Isabella took a deep breath and once again said, "I relieve you of this spell."

This time, something started to happen. Startled, Isabella closed her eyes.

"Open your eyes," said a voice.

When she did, she saw the most handsome man she had ever laid her eyes on standing before her.

Ferdinand stepped forward, took her hands in his, and hugged her before pressing a grateful kiss to her cheek.

"Thank you so much," he said. "I didn't think I would ever find someone with a pure heart that could relieve me of that terrible spell!"

They stayed in the garden, talking for the rest of the day.

"You can stay the night and get an early start in the morning," Isabella offered.

The next morning, when Isabella woke up, Ferdinand was gone. She thought she would never see him again.

But later that day, he returned, and they saw each other every day for weeks after that.

One day, Ferdinand took Isabella's hand and asked her, "Will you marry me?" Of course, Isabella said yes.

They held a grand feast to celebrate their wedding, and together, they ruled the kingdom for the rest of their days.

The End.